HO
TRANS

# OPERATION
# GLITTER HERO

WITHDRAWN

Adapted by Natalie Shaw

Simon Spotlight

New York   London   Toronto   Sydney   New Delhi

# OPERATION
# GLITTER HERO

SIMON SPOTLIGHT

An imprint of Simon & Schuster Children's Publishing Division

1230 Avenue of the Americas, New York, New York 10020

This Simon Spotlight edition December 2018

TM & © 2018 Sony Pictures Animation Inc. All Rights Reserved.

All rights reserved, including the right of reproduction in whole or in part in any form.

SIMON SPOTLIGHT and colophon are registered trademarks of Simon & Schuster, Inc.

For information about special discounts for bulk purchases, please contact Simon & Schuster Special Sales at 1-866-506-1949 or business@simonandschuster.com.

Designed by Bob Steimle

Manufactured in the United States of America 1118 LAK

10 9 8 7 6 5 4 3 2 1

ISBN 978-1-5344-3176-8 (hc)

ISBN 978-1-5344-3175-1 (pbk)

ISBN 978-1-5344-3177-5 (eBook)

# CHAPTER

## ONE

It was a perfectly spooky night at Hotel Transylvania, and Mavis and her friends were having a blast, monster style. They had turned the hotel into a giant racecourse. Now they were speeding through the halls, riding on the backs of flat, purple creatures called silverfish as if they were skateboards.

"Wheee!" yelled Mavis. "Last one to the finish line is a rainbow-loving unicorn!" she shouted at Wendy, Pedro, and Hank as they passed Bev, a real unicorn, who did not look amused.

The finish line had been marked with an eel they

had stretched between two poles from the lobby that were usually used to hold velvet rope.

Mavis was in the lead and shouted to her friends, "First place! In your face!"

She could barely get out the last word, though, because while she was talking, a zombie with a luggage cart moved into her path. Mavis slammed into it, followed by Hank and Pedro, in a pileup that seemed to end the race.

Then, from behind, Wendy passed them all, slid under the luggage cart, and beat everyone to the finish line. The eel sliced her in half in the process. But since she was a green blob made of goo, it didn't hurt.

"I win—yay me!" Wendy said, and then yelled, "Victory dance!" She danced and sang as she zoomed through the air. She was so happy—and surprised— to have won that she didn't notice she was heading toward a wall.

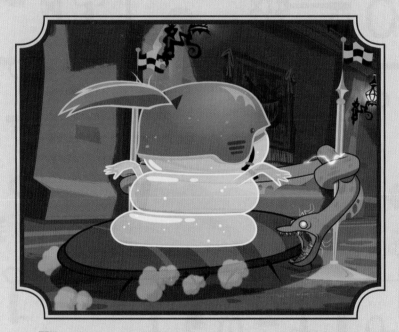

Wendy ran into it, bounced, and got sucked right into one of the hotel's vacuum tubes! They were used to take canisters of mail and other items around the hotel in seconds. A housekeeping witch had left the tube's door open by mistake.

At first, Mavis hadn't realized what had happened. "Where's Wendy?" she asked, still dazed from the crash.

Hank and Pedro pointed to green goo dripping out of the mail tube.

The tube delivered Wendy to the laundry room, where she was squeezed through a device used to get water out of wet clothes. Then she was sucked back into the tube and fell into the kitchen, where the cook stirred her up in a mixing bowl. Next, Wendy was sucked back into the tube and came out through an air vent in the lobby.

The vent cut Wendy into blobby green squares that tumbled to the ground, where her friends were waiting. It was pretty creepy, even for them, to see

their friend cut into little pieces, but the pieces quickly joined together to form Wendy again.

"How are you so lucky?" Mavis asked. "There's not a scratch on you!"

"Yeah. Well, except . . . ," Pedro began to say, but Mavis quickly signaled to him to be quiet. Mavis could see that there was a huge wad of chewing gum in Wendy's ponytail. Pedro didn't get the hint. He continued, "You know, except for that huge wad of gum in your ponytail."

Wendy shrieked. "EEEEEEEEEEEEEEEEK!" This was her worst nightmare!

Mavis glared at Pedro as if she'd been trying to say, *I told you so.*

Wendy and the gang headed straight to the hotel doctor's office. Dr. Gillman was a fishlike monster who wore goggles, a lab coat, and a stethoscope. He examined Wendy's ponytail by *licking* the gum.

"Yep, it's gum all right," Dr. Gillman confirmed. "Scare-a-mint flavor, I believe. Luckily, there's an easy fix. I'll just cut it off!" Dr. Gillman said as he grabbed a saw.

Wendy gasped. "No! This ponytail is part of me! I've had it since birth!" She thought back to when she was barely a little bit of green goo and two big eyeballs in a petri dish and sprouted her first strands of pink hair.

"There's got to be another way!" Mavis insisted.

Dr. Gillman sighed and put down the saw. "No one ever lets me use this," he said. Then he turned to the group and announced, "Fine. Everyone scrub in for surgery!"

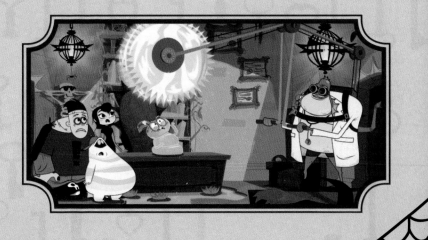

9

# CHAPTER TWO

**T**hey followed Dr. Gillman to the surgery room, and Wendy lay down on the operating table. Mavis, Hank, and Pedro wore doctor's masks and caps. They stood at the ready to give supplies to the doctor.

"Pointy thing!" Dr. Gillman said, and stuck out his hand, which was green and had webbed fingers.

Mavis handed him a pointy tool.

"Metal guy," he said, and Mavis passed him a spiky metal tool.

"Smasher," he ordered, and Mavis passed him a mallet.

"Doohickey," he said, and Mavis passed him a knife.

"Turkey sandwich!" he yelled.

Mavis passed him a turkey sandwich, and he used the knife to cut the sandwich in half and gobble it up.

"Now that lunch is over . . . ice cube!" said Dr. Gillman.

Mavis passed him an ice cube.

He held it to the gum in Wendy's hair and began to count. "One . . . two . . . three!" he said, and then he yanked on the gum. It popped right off Wendy's ponytail! "Success!" Dr. Gillman said proudly. He went out to the waiting room, where Wendy's dad, Bob Blob, was waiting for news of Wendy's operation. Bob had been keeping himself busy by knitting the fur on Bigfoot's leg. He stopped knitting when the doctor came out.

"I've got good news and bad news," Dr. Gillman said, scowling. "The bad news is," he began, "my sandwich was terrible. The good news is that Wendy and her ponytail are fine."

Bob smiled and clapped his blobby green hands. He was relieved.

Mavis pushed Wendy's wheelchair out into the crowded waiting room. Bob cried with joy. Wendy barely noticed him.

"Dr. Gillman, I owe you my life!" Wendy said, clinging to the doctor's arm.

"What?" he shouted.

"You *saved* me, and I am going to stick by your side until I can save you. It's the Way of the Blob!" Wendy explained.

Bob nodded and made an approving gurgling sound.

"You want to save my life?" Dr. Gillman asked flatly. "Invent a time machine to go back ten minutes to stop me from eating that terrible sandwich!"

Wendy looked over at her dad. "Can we, Daddy?" she asked, with a wide, braces-filled smile.

Bob shook his head.

Wendy looked more determined than ever. "I guess we're doing this the old non-time-travel way," she said.

"Fine," said Dr. Gillman.

Wendy jumped out of her wheelchair and clung to the doctor's leg. "Stuck on you it is!" she confirmed.

Dr. Gillman had no idea what he had gotten himself into. As he walked through the halls of the hotel, Wendy clung to his leg as if she were made of glue instead of goo.

At first, he didn't seem to mind. As she sang a song, he even bopped along to it:

*"Always together*
*and never apart,*
*I'll stick with you until*
*I stop a poisonous dart!"*

Wendy stopped a dart from hitting Dr. Gillman by catching it with a dartboard!

Then Dr. Gillman sang to Wendy, *"I just did my job."*

Wendy sang her reply:

> *"And you do it so well.*
> *If a ninja tries to whack you,*
> *I'll ring his bell!"*

At that, a ninja crept up, and she knocked him out of the way.

Later, in the hotel restaurant, Dr. Gillman sat impatiently while Wendy tasted his worm sundae, swallowed, and then tasted it again. This time, Dr. Gillman sang:

*"I'm sure it's not poisoned.*

*You can stop 'testing' now!"*

Wendy sang a reply, but since her mouth was full, it was impossible to understand what she was saying.

That night, Wendy stood guard outside Dr. Gillman's room, ready to protect him if duty called. She paced outside his door and sang softly:

*"Always together,*
*for your own sake,*
*until I scare off Gorgons*
*or robotic snakes!"*

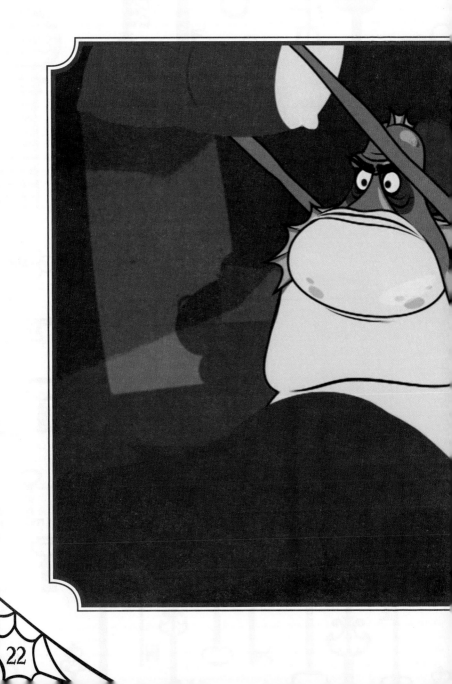

Dr. Gillman sang a reply from his bed, where he was trying—and failing—to sleep:

*"Always together,*
*I can't take much more.*
*Wendy, for the last time,*
*back awaaaaay from the*
*dooooooooor!"*

Wendy ignored him. Instead, she sang that she would stay at the door!

Dr. Gillman covered his ears with his pillow.

23

# CHAPTER THREE

**A** few days later, while in the clubhouse, Mavis tried to figure out how to break Wendy's devotion to Dr. Gillman. Hank and Pedro were busy having a burping competition.

"When is Wendy going to drop this Gillman thing?" Mavis asked. "I miss my pal!"

Just then, the skull-shaped phone rang, and Mavis answered it.

"Hello?" she asked.

"Mavis, help!" It was Dr. Gillman. He was in his office, holding up the phone receiver to one ear as

Wendy listened in through his other ear. "You gotta make her stop. I can't work, I can't take a shower...."

"Okay, hang tight, we're on it," Mavis told Dr. Gillman. "And tell Wendy I said hey!"

Wendy's eyes lit up. "Ooh, tell her I say hey back!" Wendy told Dr. Gillman.

Dr. Gillman screamed. He had no idea Wendy was right there all along!

"How did . . . ?" he began, and then shouted, "Get out of my ears!" He hung up the phone.

Back at the clubhouse, Mavis had an idea.

"Wendy needs to save Dr. Gillman to pay him back for saving her life, right? So maybe we just need to put him in danger," she told Hank and Pedro.

Mavis ran off and stopped when she saw Dr. Gillman walk by with Wendy sitting on his shoulders.

"Wendy, hey!" Mavis said casually, trying to act naturally. "How's it going with Operation Save Dr. Gillman?" she asked.

Wendy frowned. "One," she said, holding up one blobby finger before correcting Mavis. "It's called Operation Glitter Hero. And two . . . it's taking forever! He's, like, never in danger!"

Mavis smiled. "Oh really?" She acted surprised, even though she had been thinking the same thing earlier.

Suddenly, Pedro, who was pushing a room service cart, started running. He pushed the cart toward Dr. Gillman and let go. He hid behind a plant as the cart sped away.

"Look out!" Pedro yelled.

It was all part of Mavis's plan, but she pretended to know nothing about it. She even pretended to gasp when Wendy and Dr. Gillman gasped.

"Now's your chance to save Dr. Gillman," Mavis told Wendy, but Wendy was frozen in place from fear. All Wendy could do was scream! Mavis shoved Dr. Gillman out of harm's way.

Wendy flew off Dr. Gillman's shoulders and landed on the room service cart, which kept rolling down the hall.

Mavis didn't realize Wendy was in danger. "Yay!" she squealed. "Wendy saved Dr. Gillman all by herself, and there was nothing suspicious about it," she told Hank, Pedro, and Dr. Gillman. Then she

heard Wendy scream. "Uh-oh!" Mavis said, and changed into a bat.

She flew as fast as she could toward Wendy and the runaway cart, which bounced down a flight of stairs. Finally, the cart stopped when it hit a wall, but Wendy flew out an open window!

"Aaaaaaah," Wendy screamed as she fell along one of the hotel's tallest towers.

Mavis caught Wendy just in time! She flapped her bat wings furiously to keep Wendy in the air.

"Phew!" Wendy said, and looked up at Mavis's bat face in awe. "Mavis, I owe you my life!" Wendy declared, sounding as if she were about to cry.

Mavis tried to shrug it off. "What? No? That was just a reflex. A fall like that wouldn't have killed you," Mavis said.

"It would kill my adventurous nature!" Wendy insisted.

Mavis carried Wendy back into the hotel through the open window and set her down gently in a hallway.

Wendy kept talking the whole time! "But I was saved, and by my bestie. Wow!" she said happily. "Looks like I'm on Mavis watch!"

Mavis's ears perked up. "What?" she asked, looking horrified. This was not part of the plan.

A moment later, the elevator door opened, and Dr. Gillman walked out, smiling.

Wendy kept gushing about what was shaping up to be Operation Glitter Hero, Part Two: The Mavis Edition.

"So exciting!" Wendy went on. "We blobs are born guardians," she told Dr. Gillman, before turning back to Mavis, "so I won't let you out of my sight for a *second*. It'll be like a sleepover that never ends!" Wendy gushed. Then, without warning, she clung to Mavis's leg and wouldn't let go.

Mavis looked as unhappy as Dr. Gillman had looked earlier that day. Now he was full of joy, and showed it.

"Woo-hoo!" he yelled. "Free!" But he didn't celebrate for long.

"Nope," Wendy told him. "Mavis bumped me into you so, really, *she* saved you . . . and as per the Way of the Blob, I still need to repay that debt, soooo . . ." Wendy paused and pulled a bit of green

goo from her side to form a mini-Wendy "blobette." Its eyes blinked as it hopped over to Dr. Gillman's shoulder and stared at him. "Whatever my blobette sees, I see. This way Mavis and I can be totally inseparable! Great, huh?" Wendy asked.

Dr. Gillman tried pulling the blobette off his shoulder, but it held on tight. He frowned. "Welcome to my nightmare," he told Mavis.

CHAPTER FOUR

**F**rom then on, Mavis and Wendy were inseparable. Wherever Mavis went, she had to lug Wendy along, limping as Wendy clung to her leg.

El Fez, one of the hotel's skeletons and mariachi band performers, didn't help anything by playing the organ and singing new lyrics to Wendy's song:

> *"Always together,*
> *and that's the worst part.*
> *She'll stick to you like glue*
> *because of one dumb cart."*

Meanwhile, Pedro tried to stage another fake

rescue operation to trick Wendy into saving Mavis's life. He hoped Wendy would think she had fulfilled her blobby obligations and let go of Mavis.

Pedro held a chandelier by its chain, ready to drop it so it would *almost* fall on Mavis . . . and give Wendy a chance to come to Mavis's rescue.

Pedro let go of the chain and the chandelier fell . . . before he realized that Mavis had finally shaken Wendy off her leg, and Wendy was alone. The chandelier was headed straight at Wendy instead of Mavis!

Hank saw that Wendy was in danger. He dove instinctively and knocked Wendy out of the path of the chandelier.

Wendy looked at Hank with the same adoring

eyes she had shown Dr. Gillman and Mavis recently. In seconds, Wendy had stuck herself to Hank and put a little green blobette on Mavis!

Next, Pedro tried to save Hank.

When Hank and Wendy walked by, Pedro flung a mattress at them. He tried to trip Hank, giving Wendy a chance to save him.

Instead, Hank and Wendy both fell onto the mattress. Wendy thought Pedro had saved her from a fall! She put a new blobette on Hank and attached herself to Pedro!

El Fez kept on singing:

"*Always together;*
*it's like there's a curse.*
*Each time they try to stop it,*
*they just make it worse.*
*Even with teamwork,*
*they can't get it right.*
*Man, they really stink at this—*
*they're not so bright!*"

El Fez was right. The more they tried to stop Wendy, the more monsters were stuck with their own blobettes. Before long, it seemed like everyone in the hotel had one . . . even Aunt Lydia's pet chicken, Diane, who sat on hers as if it were an egg.

"Is it just me, or is this getting weird?" Hank asked. He, Mavis, and Pedro watched guests and blobettes parading through the lobby.

That was when Dr. Gillman and his blobette walked by. "Too bad about Wendy," he told them. "At least this'll all be over soon!" he hinted darkly.

"What do you mean?" asked Mavis.

Dr. Gillman explained that when a blob splits into too many pieces for too long, eventually their brains turn into mush.

Mavis, Pedro, and Hank gasped.

"Why didn't you say anything?" Mavis asked Dr. Gillman.

"Since when is it my job to warn people about

their impending deaths?" Dr. Gillman replied.

Mavis considered correcting him, but realized it was no use. She spotted Wendy attached to Bigfoot. Her friend was not looking good. Wendy had made so many little blobettes that she was now only a head, and her eyelids were drooping.

Mavis, Pedro, and Hank ran to Wendy's side.

"Wendy! You gotta pull yourself together. Literally. Now!" Mavis told her.

Wendy babbled a reply. "Not until I save all the purple cheese monkey grape!" she said.

"Uh, what was that last part?" Pedro asked.

"Horse beanie!" Wendy exclaimed, before sliding off Bigfoot's foot and gliding away.

"It's true! Her brain is turning to mush!" said Hank.

Mavis knew what to do. She went to the front desk and made an announcement into the PA system's microphone.

"Everyone with a blobette, please head to the ballroom right now for a special celebratory dance," Mavis said calmly.

Wendy's drooling head looked energized. "Ooh," Wendy said. "Me love dance times!"

"Yeah, I know," Mavis said.

# CHAPTER

## FIVE

In the ballroom, El Fez was on stage, singing, as Mavis and her blobette led the guests in a giant conga line.

As everyone danced around the room with blobettes on their shoulders, Mavis and El Fez sang instructions through their song lyrics. They said that the music would make the blobettes happy and told everyone to get ready to throw their blobettes at Wendy. As the blobettes and Wendy bounced joyfully, Mavis sang:

*"That's it! Wendy, bounce high.*
*Now let's let our blobs fly!"*

Everyone threw their blobettes at Wendy. She immediately looked like her old self again!

"We did it!" Mavis cheered.

Bigfoot was so happy that he stomped his foot—hard—right through the floor. He fell through the hole he had made, and in the process, knocked Dr. Gillman's fresh turkey sandwich right out of his hands.

"Nooo!" Dr. Gillman cried.

Wendy had something more important on her mind, which, thanks to Mavis, wasn't mushy anymore. She stretched an arm down into the hole after Bigfoot and caught him by the ankle!

"Wendy, you did it! You saved him!" Mavis said happily. She quickly added, "You saved *all* of us! All your debts are repaid!"

Dr. Gillman was still grumbling. "Not entirely," he said. "I lost my sandwich."

Wendy smiled. "Nope!" she said. "I saved that too!" Wendy yanked another arm out of the hole and tossed the sandwich to Dr. Gillman.

Dr. Gillman was thrilled . . . until the sandwich landed in Pedro's mouth!

"What?" Pedro asked when Dr. Gillman glared at him.

At least Wendy was finally free, and Hotel Transylvania could go back to normal . . . or whatever normal was for a monster hotel!